D1030912

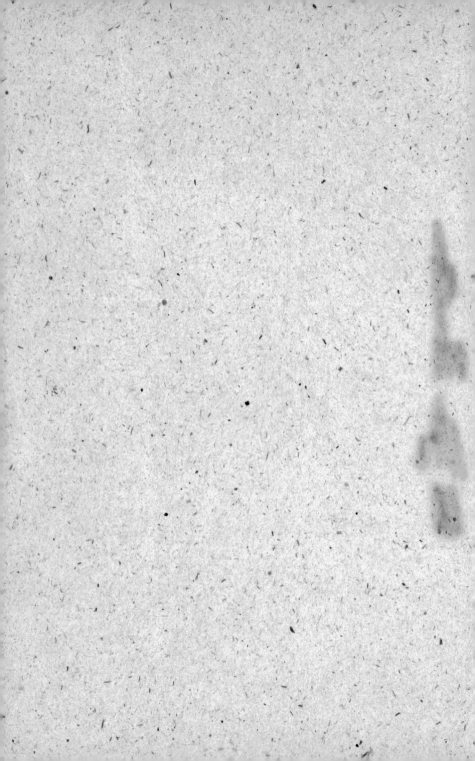

The
BEAST
of
LOR

Clyde Robert Bulla

The
BEAST
of
LOR

Illustrated by Ruth Sanderson

THOMAS Y. CROWELL COMPANY

NEW YORK

ATHENS REGIONAL LIBRARY
ATHENS, GEORGIA

J

Copyright © 1977 by Clyde Robert Bulla
All rights reserved. Except for use in a review, the
reproduction or utilization of this work in any form or
by any electronic, mechanical, or other means, now known
or hereafter invented, including xerography, photocopying,
and recording, and in any information storage and retrieval
system is forbidden without the written permission of the
publisher. Published simultaneously in Canada by
Fitzhenry & Whiteside Limited, Toronto. Manufactured in
the United States of America. Designed by Amy Hill.

Library of Congress Cataloging in Publication Data
Bulla, Clyde Robert. The beast of Lor.   SUMMARY: A series
of curious circumstances bring together an African elephant
and a young boy from an ancient British tribe.   [1. Great
Britain—History—To 449—Fiction]   I. Sanderson, Ruth.
II. Title.   PZ7.B912Bd   [Fic]   77-6751
ISBN 0-690-01377-9

1   2   3   4   5   6   7   8   9   10

To Arne Nixon

216694

Other Books by Clyde Robert Bulla

Contents

CHAPTER ONE

The Elephant

The Roman ship lay in the quiet waters of a port in Africa. The sailors were making ready for their voyage home. Some were mending ropes and sails. Others were taking on food and water. The captain had gone ashore.

He walked through the town and into the marketplace. He saw many things for sale—bowls of nuts and fruits, woven mats, birds in cages—but nothing he wished to buy. This mattered little to him. He already had a cargo of ivory and cloth to take back to Rome.

As he left the market, someone called out, "Captain!"

It was an old man in a dusty robe. "You come," he said.

The captain went with him to a clump of palm trees near the shore. Tied to one of the trees was a young elephant. It was the size of a large pony. It was gray, except for the pink in its big, drooping ears.

"Very fine," said the old man.

The elephant looked at them with small, sad eyes. It made a crying sound.

"You buy?" asked the old man.

"You want to sell me an *elephant?*" The captain began to laugh. "No, thank you! Not today!"

But afterward he thought about the beast.

He had a son at home. After every voyage the boy asked, "Father, what did you bring me?"

Wouldn't his eyes open wide at the sight of a young elephant? Wouldn't *any* boy's eyes open wide?

The captain went back to the clump of trees. The old man and the elephant were still there.

"You buy," said the old man. "I make good price."

So it was that the elephant sailed to Rome. The captain had a farm just outside the city. The elephant was taken there.

"Come, Marcus, see what I've brought," said the captain.

His son was hopping about in excitement. At the same time he was afraid. "It's so big!" he said.

"And growing bigger," said the captain. "You can grow up together."

Marcus touched the elephant's trunk. "Such a long nose," he said.

The elephant stood still.

"It likes me!" said the boy.

"Yes, it likes you already," said his father. "Make sure you take good care of it."

"Oh, I will." Marcus stroked the elephant's trunk. "I'm going to call you Longnose. I'll give you the biggest stall in the stable, and you'll always be mine!"

The boy's teacher was a Greek slave named Damon.

For years Damon had trained horses on the farm. Now he began to train the elephant.

Before many months Marcus was riding Longnose. He sat with his feet behind the beast's ears. When he pressed with his right foot, the elephant turned right. When he pressed with his other foot, it turned left. When he said, "Go," the elephant moved faster. Longnose had a funny, swinging walk that made the boy laugh.

Every day Marcus went to the stables to see Longnose. At the sight of the boy, the elephant made little snuffling sounds of happiness.

Whenever there was a storm, Marcus sat with Longnose. The elephant was afraid of storms. Once when the thunder and lightning came close, Longnose tried to break out of the stall. But when Marcus spoke, the beast was quiet again.

They grew up together. The elephant became a huge, handsome animal with fine, long tusks. Marcus became almost a man. He went on voyages with his father. He spent more and more time away from home.

He spent less and less time with Longnose.

His mother said, "The beast should be sold. It eats more than all our other animals together."

"I could never sell Longnose," said Marcus.

"As you go about the world," said his mother, "will you take the beast with you?"

"No," said Marcus.

"Then what will become of it?" she asked.

It was a question Marcus had asked himself. One day an answer came to him.

Caesar, the great Roman general, had a few elephants in his army.

"He might find a place for Longnose," said Marcus.

His father spoke with some of Caesar's men. They came and took the elephant away.

In the army Longnose was given work to do. There were wagons to pull. There were stones to be carried for building roads and bridges.

People stood along the roadsides to see the army go by. When there were young people among them, the elephant tried to stop and look into their faces.

"The beast is looking for someone," the men would say.

Once the elephant was sent into battle. It roared when spears and arrows pierced its hide. The enemy's horses were frightened.

But the Romans' horses were frightened, too. Some if them ran away. Caesar did not send Longnose into battle again. "The beast can be of more use to us in other ways," he said.

Beyond the shores of Rome lay the island of Britain. Caesar had long wanted to rule this island. Late one summer he set out to conquer it.

His army sailed in many ships. One of the ships carried the elephant.

"The Britons have never seen such a beast," said Caesar. "When they set eyes on it, they will all turn and run."

The ships sailed at night. Out of the darkness rose the island with its high, white cliffs.

The Britons were there with an army to keep the ships from landing.

The Romans sailed on, and the Britons followed them along the shore.

A little way past the cliffs some of the Romans left the ships. They fought their way across the beach. Before the second night, most of the army had landed and made camp.

The ship that carried Longnose was heavy and

slow. It was one of the last to land. After dark a dozen men brought the elephant ashore.

A storm had broken. Thunder crashed, and lightning streaked across the sky. The elephant was trembling.

"Look to the beast!" cried one of the men. "*Look to the beast!*"

CHAPTER TWO

The Witch's Child

In Britain there lived a boy named Lud. His home was a hut in the woods. There he lived with an old woman who called herself Gaim. He thought she was his grandmother, but he was not sure.

Day and night she muttered and mumbled to herself, but she said little to him. Still, in her way, she was kind. She fed and clothed him and asked nothing in return.

Once they went all the way to the village. Gaim, in her rags, walking with a skip because she was lame. Lud, in his goatskins, with his black hair falling over his eyes. Gaim had herbs to sell, but no one would buy them. Instead, people hissed at her.

She hissed back and said, "A curse on you!"

Lud hardly knew what the words meant, but he said them, too. He sang them on the way home.

He had liked the village. He kept thinking of the children who had come out of their houses to look at him and Gaim. The next day he went back.

"The witch's child!" he heard someone say.

In a moment stones were flying past him. One struck his forehead. He cried out in hurt and anger, and he turned and ran.

Afterward he hated the village, and he hid from every stranger.

A girl came to the hut. Lud had seen her before. She had been in the woods looking for herbs. Gaim had helped her find them. Now she looked frightened. She said a few words to Gaim and went quickly away.

The old woman sat in the hut, rocking back and forth and talking to herself. "It wasn't I who killed their pigs. It wasn't I who made the chief's son fall ill. No, no! I've done no harm, and I'll not go."

She saw Lud in the doorway. "But if they come for me, you must run," she said. "Do you hear me? You must *run!*"

He watched as she took a stick and poked a hole in the side of the hut.

That night he felt her shaking him awake. He heard heavy steps outside, and men's voices.

"Run!" she whispered.

She pushed him out through the hole she had made.

He ran until his legs were weak and his heart was pounding. He crept under a mat of vines and lay there.

It was two days before he dared to go back. The hut had been burned. Gaim was gone. He never saw her again.

Lud knew the woods. He knew where to hide. He found berries and shellfish to eat. At night he slept in the forks of trees, where he was safe from wild beasts.

He spied on woodcutters who came to the woods. One day, when their backs were turned, he took a knife and hatchet from their camp.

He made a bow and arrow. He knew how to make fire, and he cooked the game he shot.

It was summer, and he lived well. But when winter came, he was often hungry and cold.

He found a small cave. He made a kind of door to cover the mouth of it. The door kept out animals and helped keep the cave warm. He brought in dry leaves to make a bed. He dug a fire pit. The smoke from it went up through an opening in the rocks above.

Toward the end of winter he saw a man near the cave. Lud watched from behind a tree.

The man stumbled. He fell and lay still.

Lud came slowly out to look at him. The man's eyes were open. "Help me," he said.

Lud had become almost as wild as the beasts of the woods. When he heard the man's voice, he ran.

But something stopped him and drew him back.

The man lay there, looking up at the sky. His beard was fair and curling. His face was more young than old. It was a gentle face.

He said again, "Help me."

Lud helped him up. He led him over the rocks and into the cave.

CHAPTER THREE

Edric

The man's name was Edric. There were those who would have killed him, he said. He had escaped from them, but they had wounded him.

Lud saw the ugly gash in Edric's side. He had never dressed a wound. He did not know how to care for the man.

"What shall I do?" he asked.

"First build up the fire," said Edric, "and let me rest."

Lud built up the fire. He went out and shot two marsh birds. He cooked them over the coals and gave them to the man.

Edric ate a little. He asked for water.

Lud had made himself a wooden bowl. He took it to the stream and brought back water. Edric drank it all and asked for more. Lud brought more. Edric drank again, then lay back and closed his eyes.

Lud had given his bed to the man. He made another for himself, but it was hard for him to sleep, because he had grown used to sleeping in the cave alone.

In the morning Edric asked him, "Where are your father and mother?"

"I never knew them," said Lud.

"Are you hiding?"

"Yes."

"Why?"

Lud did not answer.

"Don't be afraid to tell me," said the man. "I am hiding, too."

"They said—they said I was the witch's child," began Lud. "They came for her—and I ran. She told me to run." He looked closely at the man. "Are you from the village?"

"What village?"

"There." Lud pointed.

"No. I come from the north."

"Is there another village in the north?"

"There are many."

"Have you seen them all?"

"No one has seen them all, but I have seen some. In my young days I was a great traveler."

"Where did you go?" asked Lud.

"North and south. East and west," said the man. "As far as the sea on every side. But never to the lands beyond."

"Lands—beyond?"

"Yes," said the man. "Did you think there are no lands but this?"

"I didn't know," said Lud.

"There are lands and there are seas, and there are more lands and more seas." Edric began to cough, and he asked for water.

Lud took the bowl to the stream. He was saying to himself, "More lands and more seas . . . more lands and more seas . . ." He ran back with the water. He asked, "Are the other lands the same as this?"

"No," said Edric.

"How are they different?"

"Someday I'll tell you."

Edric wore a chain about his neck. From the chain hung a jewel—a white stone set in a square of silver.

Most of the time it was hidden, but sometimes when he was sleeping it slipped outside his clothes. The stone was round and milky white, with little lights that flashed like fire.

"What is it?" Lud asked one day.

"Nothing now," said Edric, and he would say no more about it. Neither would he talk about himself— but he liked to talk of things he had seen in other places. Blue lakes with green islands. A cave big enough to hold every man, woman, and child in Britain. A seashore with great, white cliffs of chalk.

The lakes were in the north, he said. The cave was in the west. The white cliffs were nearest. They were to the south and east.

Edric's voice was almost a whisper. Lud had to bend close to hear the words.

He kept the cave warm. He washed Edric's ragged clothing. Every day he went hunting. Once he shot a deer, and he dried some of the meat over a low fire as he had seen Gaim do. He was anxious because Edric ate so little.

Day and night he sat by the man's bed. He listened to Edric's breathing and waited for any words he might say.

One night Edric said to him, "Go wash your face

and look at the stars!" His voice was rough, as if he were angry or in pain.

Lud went outside. In the hollow of a rock he found rainwater. He splashed some on his face. He pushed back his hair and looked at the stars.

They shone and sparkled as if they were alive. For the first time he saw colors in their brightness— yellow and blue, green and red. And the bright cloud that spread halfway across the sky—was it a cloud of little stars?

He stood there until he was cold. He went back inside.

Edric asked, "Why did you go away?"

"It was you who told me to go," said Lud. "I washed my face. I saw the stars."

"There are times when you must not listen to me," said Edric, and he looked ashamed. "I only meant— I only wanted . . ." He stopped, as if he did not know how to go on.

Lud waited.

"You are not a wild beast living out its days in a dark cave," Edric said. "I want you to lift your head. I want you to *see*. That is what I meant, Lud. That is what I meant . . ."

CHAPTER FOUR

A Journey

Spring was damp and cold. Not until summer did the days begin to grow warm.

"I want to feel the sun," said Edric.

Lud helped him outside. Edric let the sun shine on his face.

"I hear the stream," he said. "Take me to it."

They started down over the rocks, but Edric was soon weary. "It is too far," he said.

They went back to the cave. Lud had to help him at every step. Edric lay down. He was shaking as if a chill had seized him. Lud built a fire.

Edric took the chain from around his neck. He held the jewel in his hand.

"It was always . . . heavy," he said. "Here. Take it."

And Lud took the white stone and put the chain about his own neck.

That night he kept the fire burning. Toward morning he slept a little. When he woke, he went to Edric's bed.

"Shall I bring water?" he asked. There was no answer. He drew back. "Edric," he said, over and over—long after he knew his friend was dead.

He lay on the floor of the cave and wept. Still weeping, he went out into the sunshine.

He gathered stones and piled them over the mouth of the cave until the door was hidden. Then he went away into the woods.

He had his bow and arrow. In his belt he had his knife and hatchet. About his neck and hidden under his clothes he wore the jewel that had been Edric's.

For a long time he walked. He crossed a meadow. A shepherd was there with a flock of sheep. Lud ran away before the man could see him.

Back in the woods, he stopped to think. He was far from his old home. No one would know him here.

No one would look at him and say, "The witch's child!" For all he knew, the shepherd might have been friendly.

He took a road that led among farms. A woman came out of a house and asked where he was going.

"South," he answered, "and east."

First he would find the great, white cliffs. Afterward, he would see the other sights that Edric had seen.

Day after day he walked. He began to see warriors with swords and shields.

One morning he met a long line of women and children on the road. A girl told him, "We are going to the fort. We are going to stay until the battle is over."

"What battle?" he asked.

"The Romans have come," she said. "Didn't you know?"

He shook his head.

"They are here to take our land," she said. "Our warriors are going to fight them."

"Who are the Romans?"

"They are terrible men from over the sea."

"The sea? Where is it?" he asked. "Are we near the white cliffs?"

She stared at him, but she answered, "The sea is there," and she pointed. "The white cliffs are farther."

Lud went back into the woods. He walked until he saw something gleaming through the trees ahead. He came out of the woods, and the sea was there.

He looked across the hills of gray water. One after another they came in and crashed against the shore. On and on they came. There was no end to them. There could never be an end . . .

He watched until sundown. The sky was stormy. He smelled rain in the air.

He turned away from the sea and climbed a pine tree. He found a fork in a branch and curled up in it.

The storm broke. Lightning flashed, and thunder shook the earth. The rain poured, but the pine branches kept him almost dry. After the storm, he slept.

He woke with the sun in his eyes. He climbed down through the branches. He dropped to the ground and stood there, not believing what he saw.

CHAPTER FIVE

The Beast

What he saw was a great, gray beast. It had four legs and two gleaming white tusks. It had a nose like the trunk of a tree. It had big, drooping ears and small eyes.

Lud stood still and looked at it. It was part of a dream, he thought.

He moved a little. He waited for the creature to disappear or turn into something else.

It did not change. It did not disappear. When he started to walk backward, it followed him.

Lud backed away and came up against a bush. He could go no farther.

The beast gave a kind of snuffle—a small, soft sound to come from something so large. It put out its long nose. Very gently it touched his face and arms. Then the long nose curled about him.

This beast is real, Lud thought. It is real, and it could kill me.

At the same time he thought, It means no harm.

The beast let him go. Lud put a hand on its nose. Its hide was bare. It felt hard and rough, like the bark of a tree.

He looked up into its face. Its eyes had wrinkles about them. It seemed to be smiling.

All day they were together. The beast kept close to him. Lud ate some wild grain and a few berries. The beast ate, too. With its nose it tore leaves off the trees and stuffed them into its mouth. Lud lay down and drank from a stream. The beast drank, too. It drew water up into its nose and poured it into its mouth.

Lud walked all around the beast. He saw its thin tail. He saw an iron band on its hind leg.

He felt the band, and the beast turned and looked at it, too.

That night Lud slept in the fork of a tree. In the

morning, when he climbed down, the beast was waiting.

It touched him with the tip of its nose. It picked him up and lifted him into the air. Lud held his breath. The beast set him on its head and began to walk.

Lud had seen men on horseback. He had wondered what it was like to ride. Now he knew.

"Go!" he said.

But the beast was stopping. It seemed to be listening, with its ears lifted.

Lud heard footsteps. He saw men running toward them. They were strangely dressed, in long shirts and heavy shoes. In their hands were ropes and spears.

They were talking in loud voices. He could not understand their words.

One of them carried a long pole with a metal tip. He struck at Lud with it.

Lud slid to the ground.

The men were shouting their strange words. The one with the pole stabbed the beast in the jaw. The beast closed its eyes and wrinkled its forehead.

The man stabbed again, and Lud knocked the pole out of his hand.

The men seized him. They twisted his arms and

pulled his hair. He kicked and fought, but they pinned him to the ground.

Then the beast's long nose was moving among them. One of the men seemed to go flying into the air. The others ran, and Lud was free. The beast lifted him and set him on its head.

The men were closing in behind the beast. They tried to throw their ropes about its legs.

"Don't let them take you!" cried Lud.

The beast broke into a walk that was almost a run.

There was a stream ahead, a swift stream with a low bank. The beast slid down the bank. Lud fell off and into the water. He swam, and the beast swam beside him.

They crossed the stream. The beast picked Lud up, and he was riding again. He looked back. The men were on the other side with their ropes and spears.

"Go!" shouted Lud, and the beast went crashing on through the trees.

CHAPTER SIX

The Old Man

A few short, stiff hairs grew on top of the beast's head. They scratched Lud's skin. He slid back until he was riding on the beast's neck. It was more comfortable there.

They crossed two more streams. They came upon men, women, and children gathering firewood. The people cried out when they saw the beast. They fell over one another as they dropped the wood and ran.

The beast was breathing hard. It stopped to rest.

Lud caught a branch overhead and swung himself down. He found a spring of water and drank from it. The beast drank from the pool below the spring. In the pool Lud found shellfish. While he ate, the beast was eating, too. It ate all the leaves off a tree. It peeled some of the branches and ate the soft under-bark.

Lud sat on the grass. They had come a long way, but he kept watch for the men with the ropes and spears.

A voice spoke softly, "Boy—"

Lud jumped to his feet. A man was peeping out from behind a tree.

"Boy—" he said again.

"What?" asked Lud.

"That creature," said the man in his soft, frightened voice. "That terrible creature—what *is* it?"

"I don't know," answered Lud.

"You don't know?" said the man. "You are its master, and you don't know?"

Lud began to see other people. They were looking out from behind trees.

"Where did it come from?" asked the man.

Again Lud answered, "I don't know."

"Is it a dragon?" asked a child.

"That is no dragon," said someone else.

The beast was eating leaves. In the middle of a bite, it sneezed. The sound was like the crack of a tree breaking in the wind.

All the people ran, and the woods were still again.

Lud and the beast moved on. He walked, and the beast followed.

On his journey to the sea, Lud had hoped to come upon the white cliffs. He thought he must have been near them. But the strangely dressed men had been near them, too.

So Lud headed back in the way he had come.

For days he and the beast traveled together. Sometimes he walked. Sometimes he rode.

One day he made a discovery. He was riding where trees grew close together and the branches were low. As he dodged a branch, his right foot pressed behind the beast's ear. The beast turned to the right.

Lud pressed behind the other ear. The beast turned left.

"Now I can guide you!" said Lud. "Now I know how!"

He guided the beast along the trail. He saw people watching from either side. He saw them following.

They grew less afraid, and they were coming closer.

The trail became a road. It led along a stream. Lud got down to drink and look for something to eat.

People came out of the woods.

"What a great beast!" they said. "See? It has a tail in front and a tail behind."

There was an old man among them. "It is just as I thought," he said.

The others listened.

"When I was young," he said, "I saw a picture of such a creature. I saw it on a coin. The coin belonged to a trader from across the sea. He told me the name of the creature. This is an elephant."

"Elephant . . . elephant," the people said to one another.

"It has no tail in front," said the old man. "What you see is called a trunk."

"A trunk . . ." said the people.

"And I can tell you where this creature comes from," said the old man.

"Where?" asked the people.

"From across the sea," the old man told them.

"The Romans brought it here." He asked Lud, "How is it that you and the elephant are together?"

"I saw it—near the sea," said Lud. "It wanted to be with me. Some men came and tried to put ropes on it. We ran from them."

The old man nodded. "You see, it is just as I said. The men with ropes were Romans. The elephant belonged to their army, and it ran away." He said to Lud, "Bring the beast to our village. It will be a great sight for our people."

He led the way, and Lud and the elephant followed.

CHAPTER SEVEN

In the Village

Lud saw a long, high mound of earth ahead. There was a gate in the mound, and the road led up to it.

The gate opened. They went through into a village. The mound was build around it.

In the middle of the village was an open circle where a few trees grew. Lud and the elephant went with the others into the circle.

People came to gaze at the great beast. The chief was there, a rough-looking man wearing shaggy skins. His cheeks were painted blue. He and the old man spoke together in low voices.

The chief asked Lud, "Where did you find this creature?"

"Near the sea," answered Lud.

"This animal came with the Roman army," said the old man. "I am sure of it."

Again the chief spoke to Lud. "You are no Roman. Why does the creature go with you?"

"I don't know why," answered Lud.

"It is like a lost dog," the old man said to the chief. "It might follow you or me, as well."

The chief said a few words to some of his men. They left and came back dragging a heavy rope. They wound the rope about the elephant's hind legs.

"No!" said Lud.

But they had already tied the elephant to one of the trees.

Lud looked at the faces about him. He had thought they were friendly. Now he was not sure.

He said to the chief, "Take off the rope. We want to go on."

"Where?"

"Into the woods where the beast will have food and water."

"It will have food and water here," said the chief. "You must stay for the feast. Many people will be here to see the elephant."

A girl came into the circle. She was taller than Lud, and she looked older. "My name is Dola," she said. "What is yours?"

He told her.

"Where do you live?" she asked.

"Nowhere," he said.

"I live there." She pointed to the largest house in the village. "The chief is my father."

The elephant moved a little, and she sprang back. "That beast—! It is so big and ugly."

"It is not ugly," said Lud.

Dola had a leather ball in her hand. She showed it to him. It was soft, as if it were stuffed with feathers. "The girls and boys play on the hill outside the village. Do you want to play ball with us?"

He shook his head, and she left him.

Women had built fires in the circle. They were cooking meat and baking barley cakes. When Lud smelled the food, he was hungry. He sat near the elephant and waited for the feast.

Evening came. Dola brought him a piece of honey-comb on a leaf.

"Did you see Ban go by?" she asked.

"Who is Ban?"

"I forgot—you don't know him. He is our best runner. He is on his way to the Roman camp."

"Is he going to fight the Romans?"

"He could not fight them all by himself. No, he is going to tell them he knows where their beast is."

"He would not do that!"

"Why not? They are rich. They will pay to have the beast back. Ban is going to see how much they will give."

"Who has told you this?"

"I heard my father talking."

"Would he sell the beast back to the Romans? They are not our friends. They are here to take our land."

"But they are a long way from us. My father says they will never come this far."

"The Romans are cruel. They tried to hurt me, and I saw them hurt the beast." He looked at the girl's face. It was sly. She was smiling a little. "I don't believe you," he said. "I think you made up this story about a runner going to find the Romans."

"He did go."

"If he finds their camp, how can he talk to them? Their words are different from ours."

"He will draw a picture of the beast. He will make signs to tell them he knows where it is."

Lud had taken a bite of the honeycomb. He threw the rest away and started off.

"Where are you going?" she asked.

"Away from here."

He untied the rope that the men had wound about the elephant's legs. "Come," he said.

"You can't go." Dola put out her hands to stop him. "The gate is locked for the night. Come back—!"

Lud pushed her aside. He and the beast stopped before the closed gate. Men came running. The chief was among them.

"What are you doing?" he asked.

"Open the gate!" said Lud.

"Why should I?"

"We are leaving. We want no more of you and your people. You would sell the beast back to the Romans—"

"And you mean to stop me?" The chief said to the other men, "He wants to leave us. See that he does."

There was a small door in the gate. One man opened it. Two others caught Lud and pushed him out through the doorway. The door closed after him.

He beat on the gate with his fists. "Beast, beast!" he cried. "Don't let them chain you. Hear me, beast! Run from there—run!"

There was a crash. The gate burst open. The elephant came through.

"Here! I am here!" Lud held up his arms.

The elephant lifted him and set him on its head.

"Go!" shouted Lud.

The beast broke into a fast, swinging walk, and they were off down the road.

CHAPTER EIGHT

Cass

Deep in the woods they rested. In the morning Lud chose a path that led away from the village.

For days they traveled. Sometimes Lud saw people watching from among the trees. A few spoke to him, and their words sounded friendly.

He did not answer. He remembered the people in the village. Their words had been friendly, too. Then they had led him and the beast into a trap.

He told himself, We will find a place of our own.

One day he thought they had found it. It was a strip of land between a stream and a rocky bank. There were trees with leaves for the beast to eat.

There were fish in the stream. Even after sunset the bank held the warmth of the day.

He made himself a room among the rocks, with branches for a roof.

But people found them there. He saw them across the stream. Every day there were more. One was a boy in white goatskins.

Cold rains came, and the wind blew. The roof blew off Lud's room.

He saw the elephant shivering. He saw the people watching.

"Beast," he said, "we can find a better place."

They left the strip of land and set out through the woods. Lud rode on the elephant's neck.

Toward evening he looked back and saw someone following them. It was the boy in white goatskins.

"Go away!" called Lud.

The boy disappeared.

But in the morning he was following them again.

That evening Lud made camp. He saw the boy at the edge of the firelight.

Lud called out to him, "Leave us alone."

"Let me speak to you," the boy said in a strange, sad voice.

"Go away," said Lud.

The boy did not go.

"Why do you stay?" asked Lud. "Why do you follow us?"

The beast stood behind him like a great shadow. Its white tusks shone in the dark.

The boy asked, "Will it harm me?"

Lud said nothing.

The boy came slowly forward. "Have you anything to eat?"

"No," said Lud.

"I have this." The boy reached inside his clothes and took out a loaf of bread. He gave it to Lud.

Lud felt ashamed, and he did not know what to say. He broke the black, heavy loaf in two and gave half back to the boy. They sat by the fire and ate.

"My name is Cass," the boy told him. "I come from Lor."

"Is that a village?" asked Lud.

"It is a land to the north and west," said Cass. His eyes were on the beast. "What *is* this creature?"

"Some call it an elephant," answered Lud.

"Is it yours?"

"We are together."

"Is it very strong?"

"Yes."

"As strong as fifty men?"

"Stronger."

"In our village," said Cass, "we heard of you and the beast. Some did not believe there could be such a creature. But I thought it *might* be true. I ran away to find you."

"Why?"

"I heard you were a boy—a boy like me. I thought you might listen to me."

Lud ate the last of the bread. He said, "What is it you want to say?"

Cass began. He and his people lived in their land near the lakes, he said. It had been a good land, with a good and kindly king. Then the three brothers came. They were strong, quiet men. No one knew where they had come from. They built houses and walls on the cliff above the village. Little by little they gathered men about them until they had an army.

"They conquered our land and captured our king," said Cass. "We think he was killed, because we never saw him again. The three men made themselves kings, and now they rule the land. They rule by fear. They kill anyone who speaks out against them. They killed my father—" He stopped. There were tears in his eyes.

"I am sorry for you," said Lud.

"Will you help me?" asked Cass.

"What could I do?"

"You and the beast could help us rise against these men. You could help us drive them out."

"How?"

"The beast is strong."

"Yes, it is strong. But how could I tell it to drive out the three kings? It would not understand me."

"Bring the beast to Lor," said Cass. "Let the kings see it there. They will be afraid."

"And what then?"

"It will give our people hope again, to see the beast on our side," said Cass. "They might rise against these kings. There is a good man among us. His name is Baldos. He would be our leader, if he had men to follow him."

The fire had burned low.

"We can talk tomorrow," said Lud. "Now we had better sleep."

In the morning a cold rain was falling. Wet leaves blew off the trees and clung to the elephant's sides.

Lud asked, "Is it far to Lor?"

"Yes," said Cass, "but I can guide you."

"Guide us, then," said Lud.

CHAPTER NINE

Lor

For five days Cass guided them. He walked ahead. Lud rode the elephant behind him.

A little before sunset on the fifth day, they came to Lor.

Lud looked from a hilltop and saw a valley with a river winding across it. By the river was a village. On the cliff above the village were walls and rooftops rising together like a fort.

They went down into the valley. They saw a man in a field by the roadside. He stared at them, then ran off across the field.

"That was one of the kings' men," said Cass. "He has gone to tell them."

Night came as they crossed the valley. They reached the dark village.

Cass knocked at a door. A woman looked out. She had a light in her hand—a burning splinter of wood.

"So it's you," she said. "Other sons stay and help their mothers. You run away and leave me to—"

She saw the elephant. She saw Lud slide down off its back. The light fell from her hand.

"Oh, help!" she cried.

"Mother, listen," said Cass. "You remember the stories about the boy and the beast? They were true, mother."

Someone came out of the next house. A man said, "What's all the noise?"

Others came out of their houses. Some carried lighted torches. They made a wide circle around the elephant. For a while no one spoke. Then a man said, "Cass, is it you?"

"Yes, Baldos, I've come home," said Cass. "I've found the beast and the boy who rides it. They are going to help set us free."

"Will the beast fight for us?" asked Baldos.

"It will be with us," said Cass. "It will march on our side."

The men began to talk. Their voices rose.

"Call everyone together," said one.

"We can have an army, too," said another.

"And with the beast on our side, it will be greater than the kings'," said Cass.

A soldier came into the light.

"What is all this?" he asked.

No one answered until Cass spoke. "This is the end for you and your kings."

"What is this creature? Who brought it here? Take it away and go back to your houses," said the soldier. He tried to speak boldly, but his voice shook. "Quickly, before my kings hear of this. Quickly, do you hear me?"

"We hear you," said Cass, "and the time is over when you can tell us what to do."

"Yes," said Baldos, "that time is over."

Some of the other men took up the words. They laid hands on the soldier. They threw him into a puddle, and he picked himself up and limped off down the road.

There was no more sleep in the village that night. Runners went into the country and brought more men. By morning an army had gathered. Some of the men were armed with bows and arrows, others with only clubs and slingshots.

They marched across the valley with Baldos at their head. Lud rode the beast just behind him.

A man held out a spear, and the elephant reached for it.

"Look!" said the man.

A cheer went up as the beast curled its trunk about the spear and held it high.

They were on the road to the houses above. A wall blocked their way.

"Come out!" shouted Baldos. "Give yourselves up!"

No one answered.

With poles and clubs they beat down the gate. There was no one to stop them as they went on up the road.

They came to a higher wall near the top of the cliff. Faces were looking down over the wall.

"Open the gates!" Baldos called out. "Give yourselves up."

An arrow whistled past him. A spear struck the ground in front of the elephant.

Now arrows were flying past Lud's head. Something struck his shoulder like the sharp blow of a fist.

He looked down. His chin touched a wooden stick. It was the shaft of an arrow, and the arrowhead was deep in his shoulder.

He set his teeth against the pain. Baldos and his men had broken down the gate. They crowded through the opening. Lud and the elephant were with them.

CHAPTER TEN

The Kingstone

They were before the houses of the kings. The soldiers who had shot their arrows over the wall were nowhere in sight.

The army came to a stop.

"Come out!" shouted Baldos.

No one answered.

One of the men threw a stone against the nearest house. Still there was no sound from inside.

"It may be a trick," said Baldos.

A man ran forward. He peeped into one of the houses. He pushed open the door.

ATHENS REGIONAL LIBRARY
ATHENS, GEORGIA

216694

"There is no one here!" he said.

They looked into the other houses. Fires were lighted, and cookpots were on the fires. But no one was there, except for a frightened slave.

"They are gone!" said the slave. "A few soldiers stayed to hold you back until the rest could get away. The kings and all their people—they are gone, down the other side."

"They are gone," shouted the men, "and we are free!"

Lud listened to the shouts. They sounded a long way off. He put a hand to his shoulder and tried to speak. The shouting went on.

Then Cass's voice rose above the others. "Lud is wounded!"

Lud could no longer sit up on the elephant's neck. He was falling. He saw hands held out to catch him.

He knew nothing more until he found himself lying on a bed inside a house. There was something odd about the house. One wall was gone, and part of the roof.

The beast stood over him. Cass was there. About the bed stood Baldos and some of his men. They were quiet.

Lud's shoulder was stiff and sore. He touched it and felt a bandage. The arrow was gone.

"Where—?" he asked.

"Baldos took out the arrow," Cass told him. "We brought you here, to one of the kings' houses. The beast wanted to be with you. It pushed down a wall and came in, too."

Baldos came near. There was a strange look in his eyes. "That jewel . . ." he said.

Lud's clothing was open. On his bare chest lay the white stone that he wore on the chain about his neck.

"How—how did you come by that?" asked Baldos.

"Someone gave it to me," said Lud.

"Who?" asked Baldos.

"His name was Edric," said Lud.

"Edric," said Baldos, and the other men said it after him.

"Where is he now?" asked Cass.

"He is dead," answered Lud. "He was wounded, and I cared for him until he died."

"He was our king," said Cass.

"And he sent you to us," said Baldos. "He sent you and the wonderful beast to save us."

Lud shook his head. "Cass brought us here."

"I think it was the kingstone that brought you," said Baldos.

"The kingstone?"

"The stone you wear. Edric wore it, and our other kings before him. It has magic, and the magic brought you to Lor."

"I know nothing of magic," said Lud.

"But magic must know something of you," said Baldos, "that you came here to us wearing the kingstone."

He knelt, and all the other men began to kneel. Cass was already kneeling beside Lud.

Lud asked him, "Why do you kneel?"

"To do honor to you," answered Cass.

"You will be our new king," said Baldos.

"I am a boy!" said Lud.

"A boy may be a king," said Baldos.

"I do not know how to be king," said Lud.

"Baldos will help you until you are older," said Cass. "We will all help you."

Lud was very tired, and his eyes were closing. He saw Cass and the kneeling men. He saw the elephant above him.

"Beast, stay with me," he said, and as he fell asleep, he felt the elephant's trunk touch his face.

ABOUT THE AUTHOR

Clyde Robert Bulla is one of America's best-known writers for young people today. The broad scope of his interests has led him to write more than fifty fine books on a variety of subjects, including travel, history, science, and music. He has been widely praised for his rare ability to write simply yet with great warmth and sensitivity. Mr. Bulla was given the Silver Medal of the Commonwealth of California for his distinguished contribution to the field of children's books, and in 1972 his book *Pocahontas and the Strangers* received the Christopher Award.

He now lives and works in the bustling city of Los Angeles. When he is not busy writing a book, he loves to travel.

ABOUT THE ARTIST

Born in Massachusetts, Ruth Sanderson was graduated in 1974 from the Paier School of Art with a commendation as an outstanding illustration student. Since then, she has illustrated a number of books that amply bear out this verdict. She now lives in Bethany, Connecticut.

POPULAR READING

JFIC Bul   Bulla, Cly   c.2
The beast of Lor /
ATH JF   c1977.

Athens Regional Library System

3 3207 00186 2012

216694

J   Bulla

The beast of Lor

REGIONAL LIBRARY SERVICE

ATHENS AREA
ATHENS, GEORGIA 30601